Dear Parents:

Congratulations! Your child is taking the first steps on an exciting journey. The destination? Independent reading!

STEP INTO READING® will help your child get there. The program offers five steps to reading success. Each step includes fun stories and colorful art or photographs. In addition to original fiction and books with favorite characters, there are Step into Reading Non-Fiction Readers, Phonics Readers and Boxed Sets, Sticker Readers, and Comic Readers—a complete literacy program with something to interest every child.

Learning to Read, Step by Step!

Ready to Read Preschool–Kindergarten
• big type and easy words • rhyme and rhythm • picture clues
For children who know the alphabet and are eager to begin reading.

Reading with Help Preschool–Grade 1
• basic vocabulary • short sentences • simple stories
For children who recognize familiar words and sound out new words with help.

Reading on Your Own Grades 1–3
• engaging characters • easy-to-follow plots • popular topics
For children who are ready to read on their own.

Reading Paragraphs Grades 2–3
• challenging vocabulary • short paragraphs • exciting stories
For newly independent readers who read simple sentences with confidence.

Ready for Chapters Grades 2–4
• chapters • longer paragraphs • full-color art
For children who want to take the plunge into chapter books but still like colorful pictures.

STEP INTO READING® is designed to give every child a successful reading experience. The grade levels are only guides; children will progress through the steps at their own speed, developing confidence in their reading. The F&P Text Level on the back cover serves as another tool to help you choose the right book for your child.

Remember, a lifetime love of reading starts with a single step!

All rights reserved. Published in the United States by Random House Children's Books, a division of Penguin Random House LLC, New York.

Step into Reading, Random House, and the Random House colophon are registered trademarks of Penguin Random House LLC.

Visit us on the Web!
StepIntoReading.com
rhcbooks.com

Educators and librarians, for a variety of teaching tools, visit us at RHTeachersLibrarians.com

Library of Congress Cataloging-in-Publication Data is available upon request.
ISBN 978-0-593-18204-8 (trade) — ISBN 978-0-593-18205-5 (lib. bdg.) —
ISBN 978-0-593-18206-2 (ebook)

Printed in the United States of America
10 9 8 7 6 5 4 3 2 1

This book has been officially leveled by using the F&P Text Level Gradient™ Leveling System.

JOHN CENA

ELBOW GREASE

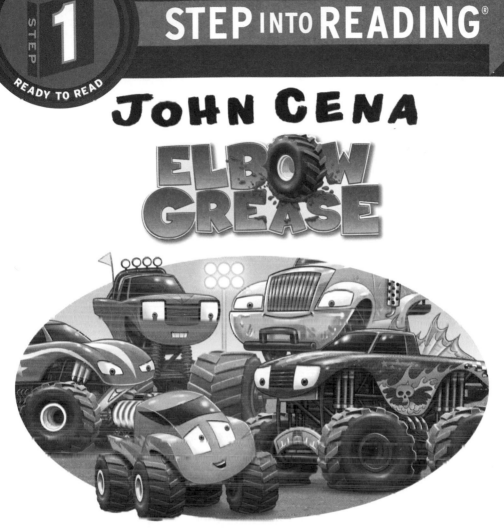

TEAMWORK WINS!

Cover illustrated by Howard McWilliam

Interior illustrated by Dave Aikins

Random House 🏠 New York

Elbow Grease
and his brothers
are monster trucks.
They love to race!

Mel helps
Elbow Grease.

She keeps the trucks
in good shape.

The trucks get
a tune-up.

Crash does not
want to wait
for a tune-up.
"Later!" he says.

The racers zip
into a tunnel!

"This is spooky!"
says Tank.

Boo!

The trucks
need to fill up
their tires!

"Hey, Crash!
Your tires need air!"
says Tank.

Crash does not stop.

"Not now!" he shouts.

Crash and Pinball
race over bumpy logs.

"Time to refuel!"

says Pinball.

The other trucks

stop for gas.

Elbow Grease

stops to charge up.

Crash keeps going.

"Not yet!" he says.

Crash slows down.

He has no gas!

His tires are flat.

Elbow Grease
and his brothers
race over to Crash.

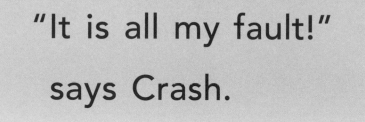

"It is all my fault!"

says Crash.

Mel and the team
will help!
Mel finds a rope.

Elbow Grease pulls.
Pinball, Tank, and
Flash push.

"Sorry!" says Crash.
"I should have
made a pit stop.
But I was having
too much fun!"

The crowd cheers. Yay!